MADGE THE MERMAID

To Jacob and Bradley,

I hope you enjoy reading my book!

Best wishes,

Stephen Parr

13th June 2018

MADGE THE MERMAID

STEPHEN PASS

ILLUSTRATED BY
JOSEPH MARC HARRISON

Acknowledgements

Stephen would like to thank the following for their help and support in producing this book:

Dr Katy Massey, Ann Pilling, Steve Wilkinson, Frank Brindle, John Sugden Steve Barton, the Bradshaws, the Pass family and last but by no means leas my wife Daniela for her endless patience, ideas and humour.

First published in Great Britain in 2014 by
Wellhouse Publications
93 Wellhouse Lane
Mirfield
WF14 0NS

Reprinted in 2016 and 2017

ISBN 978-0-9576759-0-2

Printed and bound in Great Britain by
AB Print Group Ltd, 1 Grange Valley Road, Batley, WF17 6GH

*To all the children
in the world
and all the mermaids
under the sea*

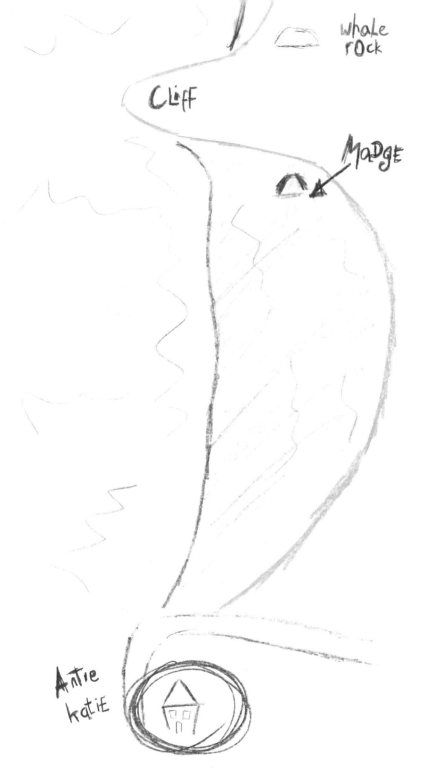

whale
rOck

CLiff

MaDge

Antie
katie

1. Madge gets her heart

When Alan first saw Madge the mermaid he gasped – she
was so colourful. She had long red hair, round yellow ears
and a purple face with white eyes and blue nose. Her arms
were also blue, she had a yellow left hand and an orange
right hand, while her green dress flowed into a long green
tail, over two metres in length.

She was standing there, looking out to sea, at the foot of
the sand-dune on the edge of the beach.

Alan ran up close to her, curious to see how she was made. He felt her wiry fish net dress and marvelled at her thick arms, which were also made of fishing netting, wrapped around a piece of wood. He shook her rubber gloved hands, laughing as he did so. He stared into her white eyes, made of plastic cups, and pressed her blue cup nose.

Then he made up a song for her:

Madge the mermaid with nose so blue

how I wish I could swim with you!

Madge the mermaid with eyes so bright

do you stay awake at night?

Madge the mermaid with tail so long

do you like my stupid song!

9

Alan laughed as he sang and then gave her a big hug, smelling the salty sea on her green netting dress. As he hugged her tight, just like he would his mum, he realised there was a difference: when he hugged his mum he could hear her heart beating in her chest but he could not hear Madge's heart.

He was still thinking this as Sammy, his auntie's black Labrador, started tugging on his left trouser leg. "Alright, alright Sammy, I'm coming," Alan told him as he let Madge go.

Sammy sprinted off towards the sea and Alan gave chase. But Sammy was fast, barking with joy as he raced along, and Alan ran and ran, ran and ran but could not catch up with him until the dog reached the edge of the sea and started splashing around in the water.

Alan eventually reached the sea, panting for breath. He bent over with his hands on his knees and his heart pounding in his ears, and he thought again of Madge and how she did not have a heart.

Suddenly, an idea came into his head as he saw a round shell by his feet. He knew what he would do - he would make Madge a heart out of seashells!

"Ha, ha!!" he thought as he began to look around the beach for shells, while Sammy ran happily around him, thinking it was a game.

But Alan was deadly serious and he had soon collected 15 shells – round ones, long straight ones, brown ones, white ones and grey ones.

With his hands so full that he couldn't carry any more, he ran back with Sammy towards Madge.

When he got to her, he started to wrap the shells carefully into the netting of her dress where he thought her heart should be.

As he did this, he sang his song once more, but this time added another verse:

Madge the mermaid
with nose so blue
how I wish
I could swim with you!

Madge the mermaid
with eyes so bright
do you stay
awake at night?

Madge the mermaid
with tail so long
do you like
my stupid song!

Madge the mermaid
with heart of shells
do you have
any tales to tell?

Suddenly he thought he heard a girl's laughter on the wind. It was a musical laugh, but it sounded distant, like it was dancing on the sea breeze.

He stopped putting the shells into Madge's dress and looked around, thinking there must be somebody nearby. But the beach was empty and so he looked up at the sand-dune and scanned the nearby cliffs, but couldn't see anyone there either.

Alan thought it strange as he continued putting the shells he had collected into the netting of Madge's dress. When he had finished, he heard the girl's voice once more, distantly on the wind:

Thank You !!

He looked around again but there was still no one on the beach, nor on the sand-dune or on the cliffs. Could it be Madge who was speaking?

He looked up, studying her face. Her yellow piping mouth was not moving, but her white cup eyes seemed to twinkle in the evening's sunlight. Wanting to see if it was her, he pressed her nose and heard the girl giggle on the wind. So he tickled her left hand and heard the giggle again!

Ha, ha!!! Madge was alive!!!

Just then his mobile phone rang. It rang three times and Alan knew that this was his auntie telling him his tea was ready.

"See ya Madge!" Alan cried out, pressing her nose once more before turning and running away, with Sammy at his heels, back to his auntie's house on top of the hill over-looking the beach. His heart was leaping for joy as he ran because Madge now had her shell heart, and she was alive!

2. Alan and Madge go swimming

Alan got back to his auntie's house and his tea was already on the kitchen table. It was his favourite - fish fingers, chips and mushy peas!

"Yes!" thought Alan. "This holiday is going to be the best ever - first Madge and now my favourite meal and being with my auntie!"

He really loved to be with Auntie Katie. She was big and cuddly and Alan found it easy to talk to her, whereas usually he was quite shy. He loved to hear her huge, booming laugh when she was happy.

Auntie Katie told Sammy to sit in his basket and, as Alan sat down to eat, she asked him about what he had done on the beach.

"Did you see Madge?"

"Yes," replied Alan, but he decided he would not tell his aunt that Madge had spoken to him on the wind. He was now nine-and-a-half years old after all and he didn't want his auntie thinking he made up little boy's stories any more.

So he simply said: "I gave her a shell heart."

"Oh, did you really," said his auntie, smiling at his news.

"Yes, I couldn't hear her heart beating so I found lots of shells and wrapped them in her dress to make her one."

"That sounds good – you'll have to show me that tomor-row."

"Yes I will," promised Alan. "She was just like you said she was."

"Told you so. Who'd have thought it when I put the broken green barrel over the tree stump!"

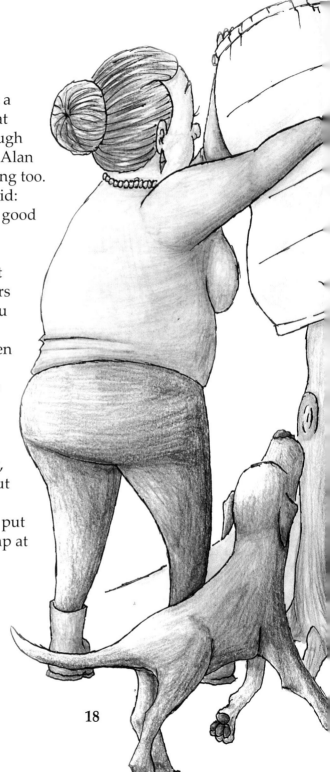

Auntie Katie let out a
humongous laugh at
the thought. Her laugh
filled the room and Alan
couldn't stop giggling too.
Still laughing, he said:
"Well, you all did a good
job."

"We did, but I don't
know who the others
were. Like I told you
this morning in the
car, I found the green
barrel washed-up
one morning on the
beach.

"I didn't want it to
be washed back out,
polluting the sea, but
it was too heavy to
carry back here so I put
it over the tree stump at
the foot of the
sand-dune for safe
keeping.

18

"Then the next morning, an old purple bucket had appeared on top of the stump - I realised someone else was tidying up the beach too!

"So I looked around for something else to add and found some old green fishing netting, which I tied onto the green barrel. Then the next day, a piece of wood appeared tied onto the stump."

19

"Which you thought looked like arms," said Alan.

"Yes, that's right. So I found a yellow rubber glove and added that for her left hand, while someone else added an orange one for her right hand. Blue fishing netting was wrapped around the wood for her arms.

"More green netting was added for her dress, then someone pushed white cups through holes in the bucket for her eyes and a blue cup for her nose."

20

"I just pressed her nose!" laughed Alan. "And I shook her hands!"

"They're very rubbery aren't they!" exclaimed his aunt, before continuing: "Well, I found a piece of yellow piping and tied that on for her mouth and next her red netting hair appeared, then her yellow cup ears and so on until she was made."

"How long did it take?" asked Alan.

"About two months in all. Her tail was made last, what did you think of it?"

21

"It's very long."

His auntie started laughing again, her deep chuckle filling the room. "It must be two metres long at least," she said, holding her arms out wide to show its size.

"It kept growing and growing as we added more and more green fishing netting. Although, like I say, I never saw whoever else was helping make Madge; we just added our bits at different times."

"Well, she's a very nice mermaid," said Alan.

"She is indeed," agreed Auntie Katie. "And you'll be able to see her again tomorrow."

They continued eating their meal in silence and Alan quickly finished – it was his favourite after all. He was then allowed to go into the sitting room with Sammy to watch TV as his auntie cleared up.

22

But he soon felt very tired – what with the long car journey to his aunt's house that morning and the sea air on his first day of holiday, he could hardly keep his eyes open. He went to bed soon afterwards and he was so tired that he fell asleep straight away.

It was then that he saw Madge again. But unlike on the beach, where she was stood upright and could not move, here she was swimming from side to side. Her round yellow ears were bent back over her head, her blue arms were by her sides and her long tail was flapping behind, propelling her through the water.

Alan thought she looked very graceful as she swam before his eyes. She did three forward rolls, spinning around in the water, giggling as she did, before she turned and spoke to him:

"Hello again!"

"Hello Madge!"

"Thank you for giving me my shell heart today."

"That's okay."

"What is your name?"

"Alan."

"Why don't you come swimming with me Alan?"

"But I can't swim."

"It doesn't matter, I will help you."

She held out her yellow hand and Alan nervously took it. He hated swimming lessons at school, where the other boys picked on him, calling him 'Baby Alan' because he could not swim. But, unlike his swimming lessons at school, where he felt heavy in the water, here he soon realised he felt weightless. He started to relax and move his arms and legs and, after a couple of strokes, he found it was easy to move.

They started off swimming slowly at first and then, without warning, Madge did another of her forward spins, giggling mischievously as she did so. "Woaahhhhh!" cried Alan as he spun around with her, his heart in his mouth.

Madge did another two spins in quick succession and Alan whooped for joy as he spun. "Woaahhhhh! This is what it must feel like to be a fish!" he thought, while Madge laughed her musical laugh.

Suddenly, Alan heard a whoosh from behind. He turned and saw a shoal of fish, like a silver cloud of smoke, appear and swim around them. The fish were tiny and it seemed there were thousands of them, darting everywhere, like five pence coins, as he felt them brushing by him.

For a minute he could not see Madge, there were so many fish, but he still felt her hand and gripped it tightly. It was now a lot harder to swim – the water was so full of tiny fish it felt like swimming through jelly.

But as quickly as the fish had appeared, they all swam off, darting as one away to the left.

"Thank goodness for that," thought Alan. It felt peaceful again and he looked over to Madge, but she was concentrating, staring straight ahead, with her yellow ears flat on her head.

Alan then heard a loud noise, a blobble sound in the water. He looked around and saw a bubble rising to the surface from below. It was a big circle in the water, as big as a car!

He peered down and saw a huge, lumbering black shadow moving about ten metres underneath them. "What is that?!" he thought and felt scared, gripping Madge's hand tightly once more.

The black shadow let out a bellow.

"WOOOHHHHH!!!" it cried out and Alan shook a little as the sound passed him by. He watched nervously as the thing passed below and suddenly he was sure it was a whale - he had seen one before in an aquarium on holiday and it had a V-shaped tail like this mammal.

As he stared, the whale let out another huge bubble from the top of its head. The bubble was coming straight for them and Alan felt scared but Madge quickly swam to her right, her long tail flapping behind as she pulled Alan along, and they just avoided the bubble as it floated towards the surface. Blobble! It went as it passed them by and Alan felt relieved.

Madge suddenly dived down, down and down, past the whale, down and down. Alan's heart was in his mouth as they descended: where was she taking him?

Down they went until Alan could see the seabed. They dropped onto the sand, which had a few pebbles on it and a mass of green algae to their right. As Alan sat, getting used to his new surroundings, he saw little twinkles flashing in the algae.

"What is that?" he thought, and continued staring until he saw that the twinkling lights were in fact dozens of seahorses stood erect, like question marks, clinging onto the vegetation. They had knobbly brown bodies and long, pointy faces and their round black eyes blinked as they swayed gently to and fro.

Madge started singing a strange, rhythmic song:

La-di-dum-da, la-di-dum-da

Dum-da-la-ha, dum-da-la-ha

La-di-dum-da, la-di-dum-da

Dum-da-la-ha, dum-da-la-ha

On and on the song went on and the seahorses started to dance, bobbing their heads up and down. Alan watched the strange display, with hundreds of heads bobbing up and down in time with Madge's song.

The seahorses then released themselves and started dancing in small circles in the water, first to the left, then to the right.

La-di-dum-da, la-di-dum-da

Dum-da-la-ha, dum-da-la-ha

La-di-dum-da, la-di-dum-da

Dum-da-la-ha, dum-da-la-ha

They danced on and on, on and on but Madge suddenly finished her song and the seahorses dropped back into the green vegetation, from where their eyes started to twinkle out once more.

Madge took Alan's hand and they started swimming up, towards the light of the surface. Up and up, up and up they swam towards the light and they were just about to break the surface when Alan woke up in his auntie's house, safe in his bed.

3. Madge makes a Rainbow Cottage

Alan went downstairs the next morning in a good mood: he had spent the night swimming with Madge and he had loved it.

It also made him feel determined to learn how to swim when he got back to school after his holidays. He would show those boys who had picked on him, calling him 'Baby Alan' because he could not swim.

As he walked into the kitchen, Sammy bounded over from his basket and jumped up at him, to say hello.

"SAMMY DOWN!!" shouted Auntie Katie in an angry voice. Alan looked up, shocked. He had never heard his auntie angry with Sammy before - she was usually always smiling and happy.

She was sat at the kitchen table with a letter in front of her, as well as a cup of tea. Auntie Katie quickly folded the letter up.

"BASKET, SAMMY, BASKET!!" she shouted as she stood up, putting the letter on top of the microwave. Then she said, in her more usual voice: "Good morning Alan….. do you want some crumpets for breakfast?"

"Yes please," he said, wondering what was wrong with her.

Auntie Katie got two crumpets and put them in the toaster. As she pushed the toaster down, she turned and asked: "Do you mind taking Sammy onto the beach today? I have got some phone calls I need to make."

"Yes, auntie, but don't you want to come and see Madge's shell heart today like you said you would?"

"Yes I do, but now I need to make some phone calls," she snapped. She looked at Alan sadly: "I'm sorry Alan. I promise I will see her heart soon."

The crumpets popped up with a crunch and Sammy jumped up at the sound, wanting to play. "GET BACK IN YOUR BASKET, YOU STUPID DOG!" Auntie Katie shouted again.

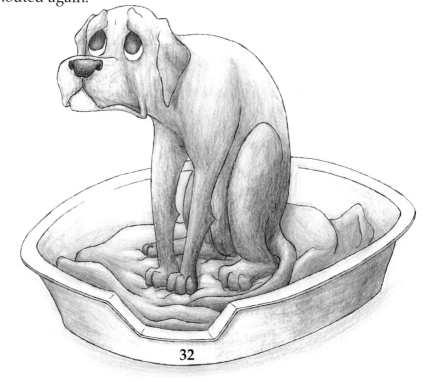

Shocked, Alan sat in silence as she buttered the crumpets and handed them to him on a plate. "Thank you auntie," he said. "Are you okay? Have I done something wrong?"

"No, no it's not you," said Auntie Katie. She let out a huge sigh. "I've just got a lot on my mind today. But don't worry, it will sort itself out, I'm sure."

But Alan did worry and he was still worrying when he went onto the beach later that morning with Sammy to see Madge.

But Madge ignored him.

He tried everything to get her to speak.

"Hiya Madge!"

Nothing.

"Remember we went swimming last night!"

Still nothing.

"The shoal of fish, the whale, how the seahorses danced to your song!"

Nothing again.

So he sang his Madge the mermaid song:

Madge the mermaid

with nose so blue

how I wish

I could swim with you!

Madge the mermaid

with eyes so bright

do you stay

awake at night?

Madge the mermaid

with tail so long

do you like

my stupid song!

Madge the mermaid

with heart of shells

do you have

any tales to tell?

But still nothing

He even tried pressing her blue cup nose but she remained silent: stood there, looking out to sea, at the foot of the sand-dune on the edge of the beach.

Alan was disappointed but he did not tell his auntie when he got home - he did not want to worry her any more or to think he made up stories.

But he worried about it for the rest of the day and was still worrying when he went to bed that night. Why had Madge not spoken to him? Had he done something wrong? Also, why had his auntie been so grumpy that morning?

But, as he lay there in bed, he also felt hope. Hope that Madge would come again in his dream, as she had the previous night.

And as he finally slid into sleep, there she was, swimming from side to side!

"Oh Madge!" Alan cried out, bursting with relief. "I'm so glad you're here!"

"So am I."

"Have I done something wrong?" he asked anxiously. "You didn't speak to me on the beach today."

"I wanted to but I couldn't," Madge replied. "You see, I can only speak on the beach if it is windy and there was no breeze."

"Really?" said Alan, surprised.

"Yes, just like I can only swim in dreams," said Madge, before she giggled mischievously: "Come on, I want to show you something!"

She held out her orange hand and Alan eagerly took it – he was not nervous like he had been the night before. They started swimming together and he again felt weightless and it was easy to move.

After a couple of spins, they swam straight down, down and down towards the seabed. Alan thought they must be going to visit the seahorses again but then his eyes made out a light shining from below. They kept swimming down and it seemed Madge was heading towards this light.

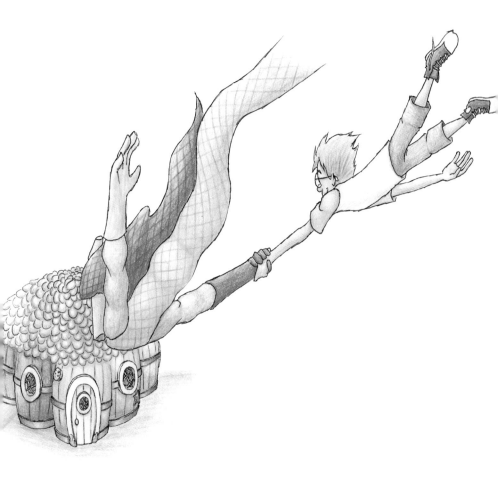

"How strange! What is it?" thought Alan, who eventually saw a silver circle on the seabed. As they got closer, he realised the silver circle was in fact a round cottage, complete with a silver shell roof!

A cottage on the seabed? Alan had never heard of such a thing! And as they swam around it, he saw it was no ordinary cottage – it was the colour of a rainbow!

It was made up of seven large barrels arranged next to each other in a circle: red, orange, yellow, green, blue, purple and pink. Alan saw each barrel had a round window. The light was shining out of the red barrel, while in the pink barrel there was also a blue door.

"Oh, I've left a light on!" said Madge, as they came to a stop outside the door. "I've been so busy today, what with making this cottage and investigating shipwrecks..... what do you think of my cottage?"

"It's very colourful."

"I picked the colours of the barrels especially as I love seeing rainbows," said Madge proudly. "But before we go in, why don't we play a game of hide-and-seek?"

"Yes let's," said Alan.

"Great! I'll count first - you go off and hide and I'll come and find you."

Madge put her rubber gloved hands over her eyes and started to count out loud. "One, two, three…" as Alan swam off across the seabed, looking for somewhere to hide.

He noticed that there was a dark shadow over to the left in the algae. He swam closer and saw it was a large green barrel lying on its side. "Ha, Madge will find it hard to find me in here!" he thought, as he swam inside and pressed himself into its darkest corner.

He waited.

And waited.

And waited.

For what seemed like an eternity.

"What if she never comes?" thought Alan. "I could be here forever."

Just then he heard a thud on top of the barrel. "Thank goodness for that," he thought, shaking a little from the impact. "She's here at last."

He looked out, ready to shout at Madge. But instead his jaw dropped with shock. For it was not Madge: it was a big shark, peering into the barrel, with its piercing eyes staring straight at him.

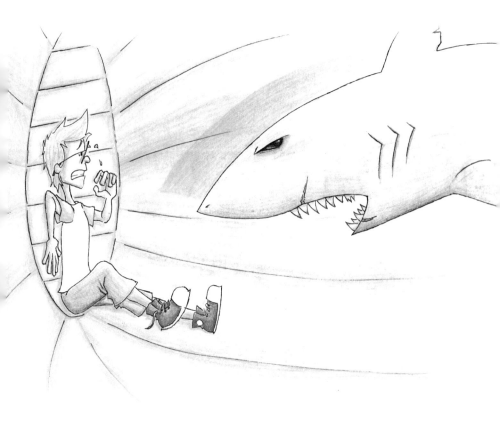

Alan looked in shock at its pointy-nosed face. The shark's mouth opened as it swam quickly towards him, exposing jagged, razor sharp teeth. He sat terrified as its mouth opened wider and wider and he could see blood on its teeth. He felt sick, his heart was pounding in his ears and he expected to be swallowed.

Suddenly he saw a green flicker appear: it was Madge's long tail. In a flash of a second, it wrapped itself around the shark, bashed its head twice against the side of the barrel and threw it far away.

Shocked, Alan watched as the spinning shark disappeared out of view.

Then he breathed a big sigh of relief.

"Thank you," he said, still shaking as Madge swam up to him to give him a hug.

"I'm sorry I took so long to find you," she said as she began to hold him tight. "You had picked such a good hiding place."

"I was very scared…. thank goodness you came when you did."

"Yes, you're safe now. You'll always be safe with me Alan – I promise."

cheese room

sea horses

tea room

gold room

RaInBoW CoTTAge

gym oo

kitchen

Bed room

4. Inside the Rainbow Cottage

Alan found it hard to go to sleep the next night: he hoped he would not see the shark again.

So he switched on his bedside light and started to read a book about a medieval wooden windmill he had visited earlier that day with his auntie and Sammy. He must have fallen asleep with the book in his hands because, all of a sudden, there Madge was, swimming from side to side, with a smile on her face.

"Hello Alan!"

"Hello Madge…. thank you for saving me from the shark last night."

"That's okay. Come on, let's go back to my rainbow cottage…. I didn't show you inside last night and I want you to see!"

"But will I be safe from the shark?"

"Of course you will - I will protect you: I promised you that last night."

Madge held out her yellow hand and Alan nervously took it. They started swimming together and Madge spun around twice, giggling as she did. Alan became so excited as he spun with her that he forgot all about the shark as Madge headed down, down and down, until he saw the silver roof of her cottage once more.

They dropped onto the seabed and Madge opened the door to her cottage, which she had recycled from a sunken boat's cabin.

"Mind your head," she said as she went in and Alan ducked as he followed her.

Madge switched on a light and Alan saw he was standing in a round pink kitchen. It was similar to his kitchen at home – it had a cooker and microwave – but there were four lobsters hung on the wall. An ancient-looking wooden table in the centre was set with white oyster shell plates, round shell cups, shell spoons and long thin sword-fish nose knives and brown crabs' legs forks. There was also a white shell jug on the table, along with cubes of yellow cheese on a platter of green seaweed.

"This is my kitchen," Madge said proudly. "I found the cooker and microwave in a small cruising yacht sunk in the rocks, while this table came from a Spanish galleon. But come on, come on, there's lots more to see."

She took Alan by the hand and they went through a door to the left. When Madge switched on the light, Alan saw he was standing inside a red room, with a bench, an anchor and six rusty cannonballs of varying sizes on the floor.

"This is my gym where I work out," said Madge proudly as she sat down on the bench.

"I got the anchor off the yacht and the cannonballs came from the galleon."

She bent down to lift up the largest cannonball, which she struggled to wrap her blue arms around, with her yellow and orange fingers only just touching.

"UUUCH!" she grunted as she lifted it off the ground.

"No wonder your arms are so thick, with this weight training you are doing," Alan said as he watched her struggle to raise it.

Madge grunted as she put the cannonball down.

"Yes, I like to keep fit, although it is a strain – I'm glad you gave me so many shells for my heart."

Next she wrapped her tail around the anchor and lifted it off the ground ten times, gasping with effort.

"This is why I could beat the shark away, my tail is so strong," she said, exhausted as she finally put the anchor down. "But come on, let's go and look at my next room."

Alan followed Madge and when she switched on the light, he saw he was standing in an orange room, which had ten wooden chests on its floor, all filled with gold coins.

"This is my gold!" said Madge excitedly. "I found these chests on the Spanish galleon. It took me ages to carry them back here, they're so heavy. But it was worth the effort as I love to watch the gold sparkle."

Alan kept staring at the gold coins, mesmerised as they twinkled under the orange light.

"Come on, come on," Madge said, holding out her yellow hand. "There's lots more to see."

She led him into a yellow room and Alan gasped – it contained a huge pile of cheese in its centre, with a small white wooden windmill to the left.

The windmill was just like the one he had seen with his auntie earlier that day, only smaller. Its wooden arms were slowly spinning around, while a nugget of cheese was being spat out of its middle on each turn, forming the pile.

"This is my cheese-making room," said Madge proudly. "I only eat cheese because I like the taste and it helps me dream. So I built this windmill to make it. Here try some!"

She picked up a nugget of cheese and handed it to Alan. He took a bite and it was the strangest cheese he had ever eaten – it tasted of vanilla ice cream!

"Great isn't it?!" said Madge as she watched Alan eat and he nodded, his mouth full. Then she handed him another cube of cheese.

"This one tastes of butterflies," she said as Alan took a bite, although he had never tasted butterflies before so he took Madge's word for it – he himself thought the cube tasted more like beefy crisps.

Madge took Alan by her yellow hand while scooping some cheese up with her orange hand. They made their way carefully around the huge pile of cheese into the next room – the green room.

It was dark in here and Alan saw hundreds of twinkles flash out at him, like stars in the night. He stared and stared and eventually saw it was algae and seahorses.

"You've brought the seahorses into your home!" he exclaimed.

"Yes!" said Madge, biting into a cube of cheese. "I like to come in here and unwind. I keep it dark and the seahorses make me happy."

She started singing her strange, rhythmic song:

La-di-dum-da, la-di-dum-da

Dum-da-la-ha, dum-da-la-ha

La-di-dum-da, la-di-dum-da

Dum-da-la-ha, dum-da-la-ha

The seahorses started to dance, bobbing their heads up and down in time with her song and Alan watched transfixed. The song went on and on before Madge suddenly stopped, took Alan by the hand and led him through the dark, through the next door.

She switched on a light and, under a low blue glow, Alan saw six large turtles on round beds in a circle around the blue barrel wall.

They were asleep, with tubes from their tails running into the top of a tall glass cylinder in the middle of the room. Blue liquid was running through the tubes into the cylinder, which was almost full.

"This is where I get blue tea from," said Madge excitedly. "My friends the turtles come here for a rest and I get blue tea – it's all I drink!"

She leaned forward and opened a small tap at the bottom of the cylinder and poured some of the tea into a shell cup. She took a gulp, before offering Alan some.

"Here try some," she said. "It's full of goodness!"

Alan took the cup and drank the tea. It tasted of fish and oysters and seaweed all mixed into one and his mouth tingled as he drank.

"Great isn't it? The taste of the ocean!" said Madge as she watched him drink and Alan nodded his head.

When he had finished, she took the cup and put it back by the cylinder. They moved through a door into a purple room, which Alan saw was Madge's bedroom. On the opposite wall, she had an ornate white shell dressing table, complete with shell mirror and shell hairbrushes, with strands of her long red hair still in them. She also had a jewellery box containing what looked like rubies and pearls.

Around most of the sides of the room was a wide, circular bed and Madge lay down on it.

"I love this deep blue colour," she said. "I love to sleep at the end of a rainbow."

Alan sat on the bed next to her and laid his head on her tail. He felt closer to her than he had ever felt before.

Madge started giggling.

"You know I like playing games," she said.

"Yes," replied Alan, remembering the game of hide-and-seek they had played the night before.

"Well, let's play sleeping logs!" laughed Madge. And with that, she promptly fell asleep and started to snore.

Her snores made Alan feel sleepy too. He fell into a deep sleep and spent the rest of the night dreaming of rainbows and gold.

5. Auntie Katie needs help

When Alan woke up the next morning, he was still thinking of Madge's rainbow cottage. Smiling to himself, he went downstairs for breakfast. Sammy jumped out of his basket as he walked into the kitchen.

"Morning Sammy!" he said, stroking the dog while looking around for his aunt. But Auntie Katie was nowhere to be seen. Then he noticed a piece of paper in the middle of the kitchen table so walked over to look. It was written in his auntie's scribbled handwriting and read:

Dear Alan

I've had to dash to the bank. Get yourself some breakfast.

Love

Auntie Katie

x

Alan thought it was strange that his aunt had had to dash off like that without waking him as he would have gone with her. But he did as she said and got himself some crumpets and a glass of orange juice. When he had finished, he thought he would tidy up for her and so washed and dried his glass and plate.

As he stood on his toes to put them back in the cupboard, which was above the microwave, he knocked the letter she had been reading a couple of days earlier. As it fell off the microwave onto the work surface, it opened out and Alan could not help noticing what it said at the top, in big letters:

FINAL WARNING

ACT NOW - MAKE PAYMENT

WE WILL REPOSSESS YOUR HOME IN

SEVEN DAYS IF YOU DO NOT

CLEAR MORTGAGE ARREARS

Alan sat down at the kitchen table and read the rest of the letter, but it did not make much sense to him. He could see it was from a bank and it was something to do with his auntie being 'in arrears'.

"That's why she must be at the bank now," thought Alan, sensing Auntie Katie must be in trouble. He also remembered how grumpy his aunt had been when she had received the letter.

Just then, the front door slammed open. Sammy jumped up barking and ran into the hallway and Alan heard his auntie's voice. A second later, Auntie Katie came bursting into the kitchen with Sammy. She was crying. Alan jumped up from the table and ran over to her.

"I'm sorry auntie, I looked at your letter. Are you in trouble?" he asked anxiously as he began to hug her tight.

"Oh Alan!" cried Auntie Katie, her booming voice trembling as she held him. "Yes, I am in trouble. The bank's going to take my house away in five days! I don't know what I'm going to do!"

She started sobbing uncontrollably.

"What's going on?"

"I lost my job and fell behind with my bills. Now I need some money or the bank will take my home away. We're going to be homeless in five days…. what am I going to do?"

"Can't you and Sammy come and live with me and my parents?" asked Alan.

"No, no I wouldn't want to do that," said Auntie Katie as she sobbed. "I wouldn't want to get in the way. And besides, I've lived here all my life - I don't want to leave. OHHHHH….. I don't know…. what am I going to do?"

But as Alan held his auntie tight, he knew what he was going to do: he was going to speak to Madge. Maybe she could help - he had seen the chests of gold in her cottage the night before, although that had been in his dream and maybe it was not for real.

But perhaps it was? Perhaps she could give him some of her gold to stop his auntie's house from being taken away.

Making the excuse he was going out to play, Alan left Sammy to comfort his aunt and he went out of the house. As he shut the front door, he felt a strong wind blowing on his face.

"Thank goodness!" thought Alan, knowing Madge would be able to speak to him on the wind.

With his fists clenched and the wind blowing in his face, he ran down onto the beach. As he headed straight towards Madge at the foot of the sand-dune, he thought of his aunt: where would she and Sammy live if they had no home? What would she do if Madge wasn't able to help?

When he reached Madge, he ran straight up to her and threw his arms around her chest.

"Oh Madge!" he gasped as he hugged her tight, gulping for air, his heart pounding in his ears. Then he burst into tears.

"Are you okay?" asked Madge.

"It's my auntie, it's my Auntie Katie!!" sobbed Alan, as he buried his face hard into Madge's chest.

Madge stood in silence and let Alan stop crying before she asked again, in a worried voice: "What is wrong?"

Alan pulled away and stared into her white plastic cup eyes. "My auntie's in trouble! Auntie Katie could be homeless – she and Sammy could be homeless!"

He started crying again as Madge tried to soothe him. "There, there Alan! Things will be okay, I'm sure."

Alan blurted out: "Can I have some of your gold please - you know, the gold you showed me in your cottage last night? You had lots but if I could just have a few coins, I could give them to my auntie to stop her being made homeless."

Madge replied straight away, her voice dancing happily on the wind: "Of course you can! I want to help! After all, I would not be here today if it wasn't for your auntie – she started making me, so of course I will help!"

"Oh Madge!" cried Alan, bursting with joy and relief as he hugged her tight once more. "Thank you! Thank you! Thank you!" and he meant it from the bottom of his heart. "I was worried that you might not be able to help because the gold in your cottage was in my dream."

"It was in your dream, yes, but the gold is real. Like I told you last night, I found it on the Spanish galleon. And as well as the gold in my cottage, there is more. You see, I do not want to keep it all in one place in case it gets stolen so I have hidden lots more coins in different places."

"Really?" said Alan, surprised.

"In fact, there are some buried in the next cove, just past the cliff: I have hidden 80 gold coins by the third rock on the right - the long, humped one, that looks like a whale. They are in an orange netting bag at the tip of the whale's head. But you will need a spade as the bag is buried deep down – I didn't want anyone to find it."

"Goodness," said Alan as he thought for a second, taking in her news. Then he cried out: "Oh Madge, thank you!"

He looked up at her face with a huge, beaming smile. Madge had told him where her gold was buried and he was going to dig it up. He turned and sprinted back along the beach with relief and joy in his heart. He was going to save his auntie's house.

6. Madge saves Alan

When Alan got back to his auntie's home on top of the hill he did not go into the kitchen as he normally would: instead he went straight round the back to her garden shed.

He opened the shed door and looked around, before seeing what he wanted among a stack of brushes in the back right hand corner. "This will do!" thought Alan as he grabbed the spade, noticing it was heavy as he lifted it out.

He shut the shed door and turned and ran back along the garden path, still without going into the house because he had decided he would not tell his aunt what he was going to do. He wanted to surprise her and started to smile as he ran, thinking what his auntie's face would be like when she saw the gold coins – he couldn't wait to see her shock and then her happiness.

He made his way down the hill and crossed the road onto the beach. It was still windy and deserted.

"Good," thought Alan, as he did not want anyone disturbing him as he dug.

The tide was out and Alan wanted to run as fast as he could to the cove, which was past Madge and the cliff at the far end of the beach. But he found it hard to go quickly as the spade, which was wooden with a metal scoop, was heavy and hurt his arm.

He slowed down, switching the spade from arm to arm as he walked. Eventually he reached the spot where Madge was standing by the sand-dune but he did not go over to her. Instead he started to walk around the outcrop of cliff between the beach and cove.

Madge called encouragement as he passed her by. "Good luck!" she said, her voice dancing excitedly on the wind. "Remember the gold is by the third rock on the right."

"Thanks Madge," he called back, his voice also carrying on the wind. "I'll see you soon!"

Alan continued on, rounded the cliff and found himself standing at the entrance to the cove. He had been there once before and walked immediately over to the right, scanning the rocks for the third one which looked like a whale. There were several small rocks and one huge, humped one.

"This has to be it!!" he thought. "Just like Madge described!"

He walked up to the rock. It had a deep puddle of water to its side and one pointy end, while its other end was rounder. He stared, not sure which end was the head. Then he remembered the whale from his dream, with its V-shaped tail: that was sort of round so Alan decided that must be the tail end and the pointy end of the rock must be the head - the gold must be there! He walked around the deep puddle and got to the pointy end and started to dig.

And dig.

And dig.

It was hard work as the spade was heavy and his arms ached as he lifted spadeful after spadeful of sand away. But he kept going, thinking of his auntie and giving her the gold and how happy she would be.

He dug 40 centimetres down, then 50 centimetres, full of hope as he shovelled the sand away, expecting to hear a clunk at any moment as the metal scoop of the spade hit the gold, or to see the netting of the bag.

With each spadeful, he eagerly glanced in the hole but there was nothing.

When the hole was 70 centimetres deep Alan paused for a second, getting his breath back. He started to wonder if he had picked the wrong end of the rock – perhaps the head was the other, more rounded end?

In frustration, he thrust the spade head down several times, as far as he could get it into the hole, but there was still no clunk of gold. But he remembered Madge had said she had buried the coins deep down to stop them being found so perhaps they were there, only further down.

His spirits renewed, he carried on digging, scooping out sand bit by bit, hoping for the clunk or at least to see the orange netting bag. The spade was heavy and he dug another 30 centimetres down but still there was nothing. He thrust the spade into the hole again in desperation.

Still no clunk.

"Oh no! I must have picked the wrong end," he thought and debated whether he should run back to Madge and ask her but he saw the tide was coming in and there was no time.

The gold had to be at the other end of the whale rock and he had to find it!

Tired, he stumbled around the puddle with the spade and started digging at the round end.

But he worked slowly as his arms were aching and he had only got 30 centimetres down when he decided to ditch the heavy spade and use his bare hands, kneeling into the hole as he scooped the wet sand out.

Scoop after scoop he dug and he eventually got to 60 centimetres down but there was still no orange bag or gold. Then he heard Madge's voice, sounding worried on the wind.

"Alan, Alan, where are you?" she asked. "You must stop now, the tide is coming in!"

Alan looked around, exhausted. The tide was almost at the entrance to the cove. But he had to have the gold and he was sure it was there.

So he knelt back into the hole and started scooping more sand out.

"Where is it? Where is it? Come on, come on!!!" he thought as he heaved sand out.

He dug out ten more handfuls when suddenly he felt some netting with the little finger of his left hand. He looked down and saw netting covered in sand but he could make out it was orange.

"YESSSSSSSSSSSSSSS!!!!" he thought.

With a renewed energy in his arms he frantically dug down, around the bag to try and release it. Then he heard Madge's voice once more on the wind. It was more urgent: "Alan! Alan! Come on, you must come NOW!"

He felt some water lap his trainers and he realised the tide was upon him. He felt shivers of fright run down his spine, but he had to have the bag.

He grabbed at it with one hand and dug around it with the other. Finally, he freed the bag, before hauling it out of the hole.

It felt heavy as he lifted it out, but he saw a glint of gold through the orange netting!

"YES!!!! MY AUNTIE'S HOUSE WILL BE SAVED!" he thought, and let out a whoop of joy before turning to get out of the cove. But the water was now up to his ankles as he splashed through it and he decided to leave the spade on the sand, there was no time!

He walked out into the sea to get around the cliff and out of the cove, splashing through the water until he was up to his knees.

He was scared as he walked. He could not swim and did not like the water around him. But he struggled on, splashing his way around the outcrop of rocks. At last, he could see Madge in the distance. But the tide was still coming in and he did not think he could reach her.

So he decided to try and climb the cliff.

He walked up to a nearby ledge and, holding the gold out
of the water with his left hand, he grabbed on with his
right hand and tried to haul himself up, pressing down
hard with his right foot.

He pushed and grabbed and raised himself out of the sea
but his foot slipped and he fell back into the water, scrap-
ing his foot and splashing down. The water covered his
head as he crashed back down and he breathed some
water in through his nose and panicked.

"I am going to drown!" he thought, terrified.

But somehow he managed to stand up again, still holding onto the bag of gold and with his glasses still on his face. His right foot was aching from his fall and, disorientated, he looked around to get his bearings. Madge screamed at him on the wind:

"Alan, come to me, RIGHT NOW. You can do it - come on, come quickly."

Alan was terrified. He was stood up to his waist in the sea with Madge still far away. She shouted again:

"Alan, walk to me! NOW!! You can do it!"

He fixed his stare on Madge's face, concentrating on her blue nose as he started wading through the water towards her. The gold weighed him down and he was getting cold and was very scared but Madge kept shouting encouragement:

"Keep going Alan, you are almost here! You can do it, keep going!"

Shivering with the cold and fright, Alan kept walking until he saw the green tip of Madge's tail in the sea.

"Look, here is my tail, GRAB ONTO MY TAIL!" Madge shouted.

Alan threw himself forward and managed to just grab hold of it. Using the last of his strength, he climbed up the netting of her tail and dress and hauled himself onto her right arm, where he sat exhausted, hugging onto Madge.

He was still clutching the bag of gold. And he was safe.

7. Alan and Madge confess

Alan did not know how long he had been asleep but the
tide was going out when he woke up. He was still holding
onto Madge and the bag of gold.

He heard shouting and barking and looked up to see his auntie standing on top of the sand-dune, while Sammy was racing down towards him.

"Alan! Oh Alan!" his auntie cried out as Sammy got to the bottom of the sand-dune and started jumping up excitedly. Auntie Katie followed and soon reached Alan and she lifted him off Madge's right arm before sitting down and cuddling him, while Sammy licked his face.

"Oh Alan – you're safe, thank God you're safe!" she said, her booming voice trembling. She was so relieved to see him, she did not notice he was holding the bag of gold.

"Where have you been? I've been worried sick!" she said, while also pushing Sammy away. "Sammy sit down, give Alan space!"

Alan looked up at his auntie, feeling better for seeing her, as well as from the warmth of her body as she cuddled him tight.

"I went to find some gold," he said and lifted the orange bag of gold up from his lap.

"This is for you."

Auntie Katie's eyes widened in wonder at what she saw: the glint of dozens of gold coins in the afternoon sun.

"Wha...where did you find that?" she asked, flabbergasted.

"Madge told me where it was. I found it in the cove. Your house is safe now."

"Asked Madge…?" said Auntie Katie, her voice confused.

"I go swimming with Madge in my dreams, and she has lots of gold in her rainbow cottage under the sea – I asked if I could have some."

"It is true," said Madge, her voice dancing excitedly on the wind. "I wanted to help."

Auntie Katie sat in stunned silence for a moment. Then she cried out: "Who was that – was that Madge speaking?"

"Yes auntie – Madge can speak on the wind! She talks on the wind!"

Auntie Katie looked up at Madge in shock and wonder.

Alan went on: "She started to speak when I gave her her shell heart. I didn't want to tell you as I didn't want you to think I made up stories. I'm sorry to have kept it a secret."

"Blimey," said Auntie Katie, her voice stunned.

"Well, Madge found some gold on a sunken Spanish galleon and let me have some – she told me it was hidden in the next cove. So I took your spade from the shed and went to dig it up. But I got confused as to which end of the whale rock she had hidden it so it took much longer than I thought.

"The tide came in and I was very scared and I hurt my right foot trying to climb up the cliff. I fell back into the sea but Madge saved me with her tail, I managed to climb up her tail!"

Auntie Katie sat stunned, taking in what she had heard. Then she cried out: "You stupid boy! You can't swim! What were you thinking of! You could have drowned!"

But Madge spoke up in Alan's defence.

"It was my fault," she said. "I did not explain properly to Alan which end of the whale rock the gold was buried. He got the gold for you, to save your home."

Auntie Katie thought for a moment and nodded her head.

"Yes you're right, he did," she said, before she leant over Alan and untied the lace on his right trainer, lifting the shoe off his foot as gently as she could. But Alan still let out a shout of pain.

"I'm sorry, I'm sorry," said Auntie Katie, as she took off his bloodied sock to reveal a four centimetre cut on the top of his foot from where he had fallen.

"Ah, the cut's not too deep," she said, relief in her voice. "I've got a first aid kit at home and I will bandage it after you've had a bath. We'll soon have you mended!"

"Yes auntie," said Alan, before he anxiously blurted out: "I'm sorry but I lost your spade as the tide came in – I couldn't carry it and the gold."

"It doesn't matter, I'm just glad you're safe," said his aunt, as she put his sock and trainer back on. Alan flinched as she did so.

"It's a good job too - I'm taking you home tomorrow, what would your mum and dad say!"

Auntie Katie let out one of her humongous laughs.

"I still can't believe it Alan….. what you've told me, what you did."

She then kissed him on his forehead.

"You didn't come home for your lunch and I was worried sick where you were. I tried ringing you on your phone but you've left it in your bedroom. So I set off with Sammy across the sand-dunes to find you.

"Come on, let's get you home."

She placed Alan gently onto the sand and got up, with Sammy jumping up and again licking his face.

"Sammy, down, down! Alan's had enough excitement for one day!" she said as she lifted Alan up onto his feet.

"Right Alan, I'm going to give you a piggyback home, you need to save your foot."

She leant forwards and Alan climbed onto her back, still holding the bag of gold.

"See ya Madge," Alan said, still exhausted from his adventure.

"Yes, see you Madge," said Auntie Katie, her booming voice now sounding cheery. "And thank you for saving Alan. Thank you also for the gold."

"That's okay," said Madge. "Thank you for helping make me."

8. Alan says goodbye

Alan eventually woke up the next morning feeling very rested, like he had slept forever. As he lay in bed, gently moving his foot around to see if it was okay, he heard his auntie coming up the stairs.

"Good morning Alan! My goodness, you've slept for such a long time!" said Auntie Katie cheerily as she came bursting into the bedroom, carrying a tray with a bacon sandwich and a glass of orange juice.

"I thought I would give you breakfast in bed seeing as it's your last day of holiday. A good breakfast and then we'll be on our way. How is your foot…. how is the bandage?" she said as she put the tray down on the bedside table and lifted the duvet to look.

"It hurts a little but it's okay," said Alan as he turned his foot around to show her. "Please auntie, can I go and say goodbye to Madge before we go?"

"Of course you can! And will you thank her again for the gold – I counted it last night and there are 80 gold coins, it will easily save my house!"

Auntie Katie let out a humongous laugh and Alan started giggling too, he was glad she was happy again.

After eating his breakfast, he got ready and went with Sammy onto the windy beach. His foot hurt as he walked but he kept going and finally reached Madge by the sand-dune.

"Hiya Madge!" he said.

"Hello Alan. How are you today?"

"Okay thanks, my foot is hurting but I can walk on it."

"That is good."

"I was so exhausted I didn't see you when I fell asleep last night, did we go swimming together in my dream?"

"No. You had had such a long day I decided to leave you alone to have a good rest. I did some weightlifting and sat with the seahorses instead. Look, I've got a present for you, it's by my tail."

Alan looked down and saw a shell teacup with some blue tea in it.

"Drink the tea Alan – it is very good for you. It has the goodness of the ocean in it and it will help your foot recover."

Alan picked the cup up and gulped the tea down. The tea made him feel instantly better and his foot no longer hurt.

"Thanks," he said with a grin on his face as he put the cup down and turned to face Madge.

"I'm going back to my home today – back to see my parents. But can we still go swimming together in my dreams while I am away?"

"Yes, of course we can."

"I'm going to learn how to swim for real as well when I get home to stop the bullies at school from calling me 'Baby Alan'."

"Why do they do that?"

"Because I am nine-and-a-half years old and I can't swim."

"Yes you can Alan – if you can walk through the sea and swim with me in your dreams, you can learn how to swim. It is easy, you just have to put your arms together, kick your legs and believe in yourself."

"I suppose so, yes."

"Go for a swim now, Alan, I will watch you and keep you safe. Don't go in too deep and practise a few strokes. You can do it. You can then dry yourself on my tail."

Alan looked around and the beach was deserted.

"Why not?" he thought, feeling determined that he could do it. But his heart was still in his mouth as he took his clothes and glasses off and ran down to the sea, with Sammy racing ahead of him, barking.

The water was cold as he put his foot in and he felt scared but he knew Madge was watching. So he waded into the sea, with Sammy swimming by him.

"You can do it!" Madge shouted on the wind and with that, Alan took a deep breath and plunged his head under and tried to swim.

He moved his arms and kicked his legs like Madge had said and found he could float.

"Whooppee!!!!" he thought as he swam a few metres.

"Well done!!" shouted Madge on the wind.

Feeling a surge of delight and excitement, Alan swam back and forth a few times, loving the feeling of being able to float, move and turn in the water.

When he finally stopped and stood up, he waved to Madge in delight.

"Well done!!" Madge shouted again. "You did it!!"

Alan suddenly remembered he had to get back to his aunt's, so he reluctantly got out of the sea and ran back to Madge, with Sammy at his heels. His heart was leaping for joy as he ran. "I can swim, I can swim!!" he kept saying to himself, and he felt a great sense of achievement.

"Did you enjoy that?" asked Madge as he reached her.

"I loved it!!" said Alan as he started to dry himself on her tail. "I'll show those bullies when I get home I'm not 'Baby Alan' anymore!"

Once dry, Alan put his clothes and glasses back on…

90

… and gave Madge a big hug, singing his song once more, laughing as he held her tight:

Madge the mermaid

with nose so blue

now I can

swim with you!

Madge the mermaid

with eyes so bright

we like to swim

together at night!

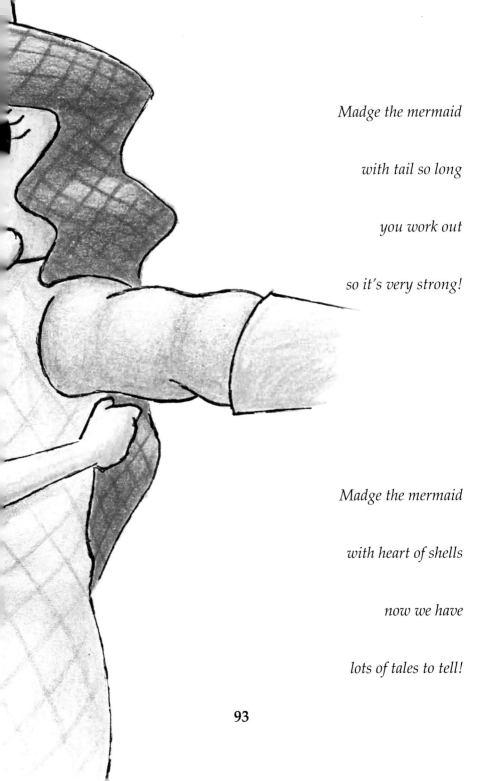

Madge the mermaid

with tail so long

you work out

so it's very strong!

Madge the mermaid

with heart of shells

now we have

lots of tales to tell!

93

Madge giggled in delight on the wind as he sang and when he had finished, he kissed her on the cheek and pressed her blue cup nose before he turned and started running back to his auntie's house with Sammy.

He was sad to be leaving but he had had an excellent holiday. He had met Madge, saved his auntie's house and now he had learned how to swim!

When he got about halfway along the beach, he stopped and turned and waved at Madge. "See ya Madge, see you soon!" he shouted on the wind.

"Bye bye Alan!"

Alan turned and kept running with Sammy. When he got to his auntie's house, she was already outside, waiting by her car.

"I can swim auntie!" said Alan, bursting with pride as he ran up to give her a big hug.

"I just watched you," said Auntie Katie, her booming voice sounding delighted as she cuddled him. "Well done Alan!!"

They held each other tight for a minute.

"I'm going to miss you auntie, can I come to stay with you again soon please?"

"Yes, of course you can! And I will miss you too!"

Auntie Katie had already packed the car and they got in and set off. As Alan lay on the back seat, looking at his aunt and Sammy in the front, he suddenly felt sleepy, what with the blue tea and swimming in the sea.

He fell asleep and there was Madge, swimming from side to side.

He was so happy. His and Madge's adventures would continue!